www.mascotbooks.com

Texas Farm Girl: Reap What You Sow

For more information, please contact:
Mascot Books
560 Herndon Parkway #120
Herndon, VA 20170
info@mascotbooks.com

Library of Congress Control Number: 2014918603

CPSIA Code: PRT1114A
ISBN-13: 9781620862636

Printed in the United States

Texas Farm Girl

Reap What You Sow

Written by:
Rebecca Crownover

Illustrations by:
Brian Daigle

After working for my PawPaw a couple of years at the farm, plowing fields, and driving grain carts during harvest, he asked me to do something I had not done before. "How would you like to plant a corn field, Texas Farm Girl?"

Grain Cart: Trailer with a bin that is pulled by a tractor that allows the combine to dump harvested grain into it while in the field.

Harvest: The time of year when the crops are ready to be taken from the field.

I was so excited! I had never planted a crop before. I had only plowed the dirt with a plow to get it ready to plant. This was a new opportunity to do an important task— plant corn! "Yes! I would love to plant corn, PawPaw!"

Plow: Farm equipment that is pulled by a tractor that digs into and turns the soil over to prepare the soil for planting. Once the soil has been plowed, the field can be planted.

I already knew how to drive a tractor, but using a planter was different. PawPaw spent some time explaining to me exactly what I needed to do. "Planting the seeds for a new crop is a very important job," he said. "You will need to fill the planter boxes with corn seed.

When driving the tractor, you must drive it in a straight line.

Do not get impatient and drive too fast! It's important to take your time and pay attention to detail to do a good job."

"As you plant, it is also important to get out of the tractor and check the planter boxes on the planter and add corn seed when they get low. If you run out of corn seed in the planter box, then corn will not get planted."

Planter: Farm equipment that is pulled by a tractor with planter boxes that are used to plant (sow) seeds into the soil.

PawPaw rode with me on the tractor as we planted the corn seed until he was happy that I understood how to plant. He gave me the responsibility to plant the rest of this field and I was tickled pink! It took me four days to plant this field of corn.

At the end of the four days, I had some bags of corn seed leftover. I didn't think too much about it, but PawPaw was concerned that I had seed left. He thought he had calculated exactly how much seed was needed to plant that field.

A few weeks later the corn began to grow. PawPaw and I noticed something. Looking down the planted rows, there were rows where corn was not growing.

"Oh no!" exclaimed PawPaw. "Some of the planter boxes must have run out of seed and there are a number of rows that did not get planted. That's why there were extra seed bags leftover."

Rows: Rows are lines of corn that have been planted.

At that moment, my heart sank. I knew I had made a mistake. I got so comfortable planting and listening to my music in the tractor that I became careless and allowed the planter boxes to run out of seed before I re-filled them, planting nothing on so many rows.

PawPaw was disappointed in me for not listening, but instead of yelling at me for making a mistake, he sat me down right there in the field.

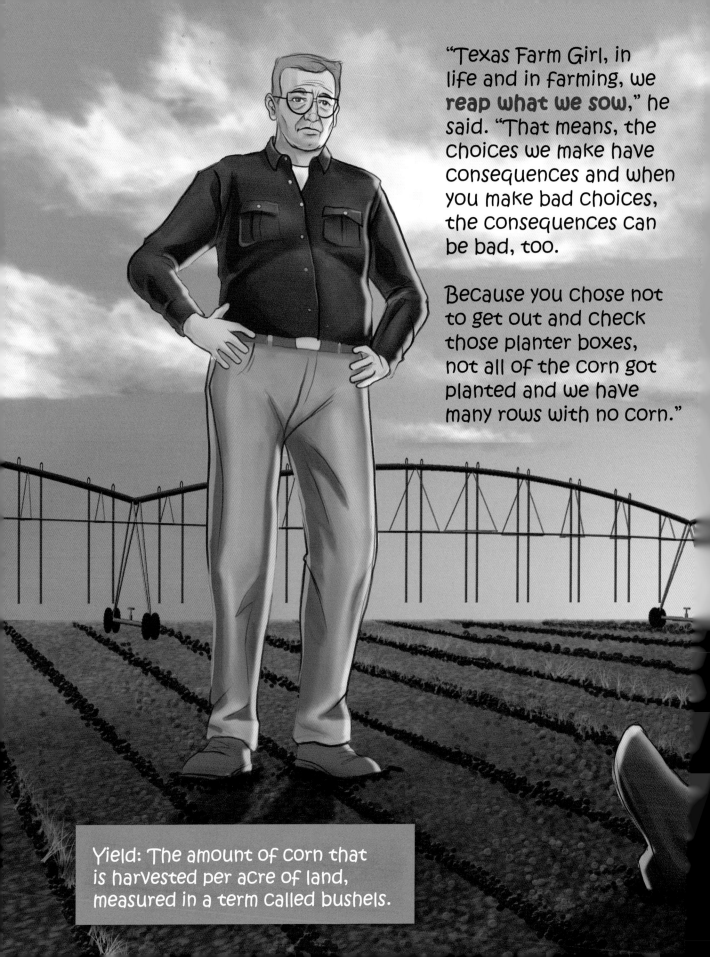

"Texas Farm Girl, in life and in farming, we **reap what we sow**," he said. "That means, the choices we make have consequences and when you make bad choices, the consequences can be bad, too.

Because you chose not to get out and check those planter boxes, not all of the corn got planted and we have many rows with no corn."

Yield: The amount of corn that is harvested per acre of land, measured in a term called bushels.

"The consequence of that decision is that it is going to cost the farm money by purchasing more corn seed to replant and extra time to plow the field in order to replant it. It will also cause the corn to be planted late and may also cause the yield to be less if it gets too cold before harvest time. You see, Texas Farm Girl, you must not take things I teach you for granted. Just like your parents, I want to teach you the things that will help you do a good job so you can Shine Like a Lone Star Pearl."

Shine Like a Lone Star Pearl: Shining like a pearl through hard times by turning a negative into a positive, Texas style.

PawPaw told me I would have to **reap what I had sown.**
"You and I are going to have to work from sunrise to
sunset until we get this field of corn replanted."

"I will drive a tractor with the plow to prepare the dirt and you can plant the new corn seed behind me. We have a very short window of opportunity because now this field will be planted late."

I understood what I had done wrong and what I needed to do to make it right to **Shine Like a Lone Star Pearl.** I got to work immediately and the first thing I did was make sure all of the planter boxes were full of seed.

I also checked the planter boxes often and took my time to do a good job to get all of the corn seed planted right.

Harvest time came and we had to wait a few weeks longer to harvest the field of corn that I had replanted. When we cut the corn that I had replanted, it turned out to be as good as if we planted it on time.

Just as we finished harvesting the field, a big winter storm moved in with freezing temperatures. Thankfully we were able to harvest the corn when we did. If it had been any later, it would have damaged the corn yield and lost the farm even more money.

When the air temperature drops to 32°F or below for 4+ hours, the cold temperature can kill or severely damage the corn plant.

"I am proud of you, Texas Farm Girl.
Although you made a mistake the first time,
you did the right thing by working hard to get
the field replanted before it was too late."

"By taking responsibility for your mistake and making it right, you were able to plant a good crop after all and save the farm from losing more money."

I learned a big lesson from that experience. I let my PawPaw down and lost his trust in me. I lost the farm money and time. I had to work extra-long days to replant the field of corn. But in the end, by taking responsibility for my mistake, I was able to gain PawPaw's trust back and show him that I was capable of planting corn and that I could **Shine Like a Lone Star Pearl.**

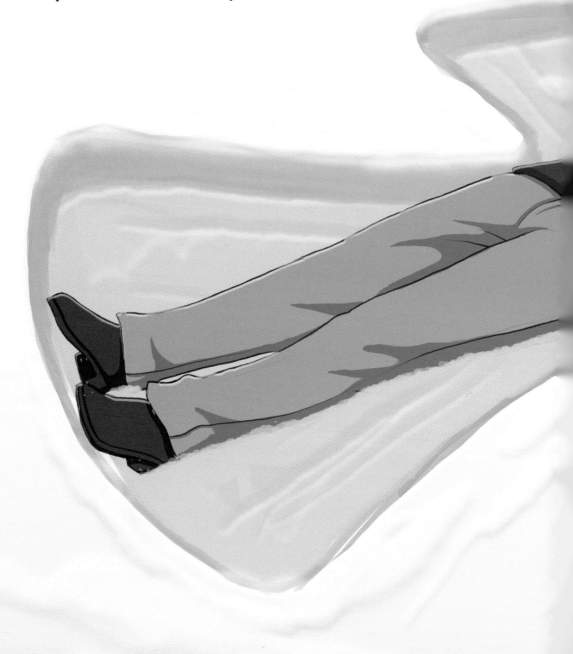

I realized that paying attention to detail is important. Listening to my PawPaw's directions and obeying what he said was even more important.

Learning a lesson the hard way isn't very fun and can be costly. Sometimes we don't think how our decisions can affect ourselves and others. **Reap what you sow** is one lesson I will never forget!

I am thankful my PawPaw still loves me and was able to give me guidance that will help me **Shine Like a Lone Star Pearl** the rest of my life.

Questions for the reader:

Can you think of a time where you reaped what you sowed?

Did you do something right or something wrong?

Did it bring joy or sadness?

If it was a bad choice you made, what did you do to make it right?

What lesson did you learn?

From the Author

I'll never forget the summer of 1995 when I planted a corn crop for my PawPaw that didn't come up because I wasn't paying attention to the planters. It truly did impact my PawPaw's farm costs—and my grandma's shopping budget—that year by the extra that was incurred to replant the crop.

Today, tractors are more sophisticated with monitors and alerts that will tell you if your planter boxes are getting low or out of seed to prevent this situation from happening. However, we can still make mistakes in farming and in life regardless of the technology that surrounds us if we are not paying attention.

Why do farmers plant seeds? Because they expect to reap (harvest) a bigger number than they sow (plant). A single kernel can yield hundreds of seeds. It is the same way with our own lives. A small decision to do either good or bad reaps a much bigger crop, for either happiness or sadness. If we sow good seeds in life by always doing our best, being positive, and doing the right thing, we will reap the benefits of those decisions at a later date. I like to call those rewards of blessings. Of course, if we choose the opposite, we take away our opportunities for blessings of joy.

Since that summer of 1995, I have used that experience as a valuable lesson in my life to always pay attention to detail and to listen carefully to directions so that I am always making the best possible decisions. And when I do make mistakes or happen to make the wrong choice, I always work hard to make it right. Doing what my PawPaw taught me about reaping what I sow has been a life lesson that has given me an edge of success in many situations.

May my hard lesson learned be a lesson to you to always do your best and make the best possible decisions in your life. If you do make a mistake, do what it takes to make it right. And if you want to do it Texas style, you will Shine Like a Lone Star Pearl.

-Rebecca Crownover

Rebecca Crownover, a true entrepreneur: a farmer by profession as partner in a family farm, an Award Winning Children's Book Author, and founder of the brand and children's books, Texas Farm Girl. Rebecca writes children's books with purpose behind them based on her own life experiences.

Born and raised in the Texas Panhandle, Rebecca Crownover grew up in Sunray, Texas, a small farming community. Her grandfather was a farmer, and through her junior high and high school years she worked on the farm in the summers driving tractors and helping out with irrigation. Her experiences working with her grandfather on the farm sets the stage for Texas Farm Girl to educate, entertain, and inspire children with life lessons through farming.

Rebecca got her start as a Children's Book Author by publishing the book *My Daddy Is In Heaven With Jesus*, an award-winning children's book that helps children find comfort after losing a parent. Based on her own personal tragedy of losing a husband at the young age of 31 and her daughter losing her father at 2 ½ years of age, Rebecca has inspired many through her work.

To learn more about the author, visit:
rebeccacrownover.com

To learn more about Texas Farm Girl, visit:
texasfarmgirl.com

Have a book idea?

Contact us at:

Mascot Books

560 Herndon Parkway

Suite 120

Herndon, VA

info@mascotbooks.com | www.mascotbooks.com